THE PIG IN A WIG

小豬戴假髮

Alan MacDonald 著

Paul Hess 繪

施純宜 譯

三民書局

Once some animals lived on a farm in a **humble**, **tumbledown** barn. One of them was a pig called Peggoty. Peggoty was a kind-hearted pig, but she was rather proud of her looks and she would spend hours **admiring** her **reflection** in the duck pond. She secretly believed herself to be the prettiest, pinkest, most perfect pig in all the world.

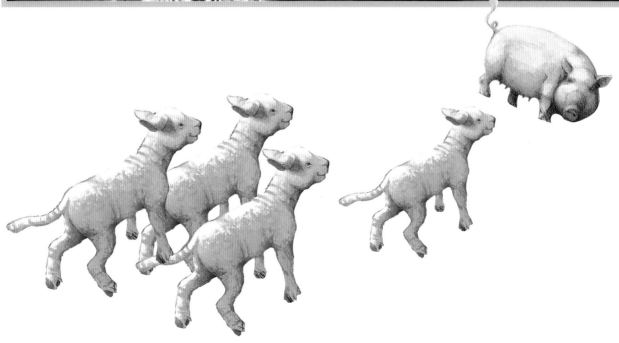

從前，有一群動物住在一間破破爛爛、快要倒塌的穀倉裡。其中有一隻小豬，叫做佩葛蒂。心地善良的佩葛蒂對自己的容貌感到十分驕傲，常常花好多時間待在鴨子的水塘邊，陶醉地欣賞自己的倒影。她暗暗相信自己是全世界最漂亮、最粉嫩、最完美的小豬。

One spring morning some young lambs passed
the farmyard gate on their way to the fields.
Peggoty was **gazing** at herself in the duck pond as
usual. The lambs stopped to **stare** at her. They were
very pleased with their new woolly coats and hadn't
yet learned any manners.

"Look at the fat ol' pig," said one.

"Look at her big snorty snout."

"Isn't she ugly?" they said.

Peggoty didn't hear them,
until one lamb started to **bleat** a song
and the others joined in.

"Ugly ol' pig, bet you smell,
You're pink and fat
and you're **bald** as well!"

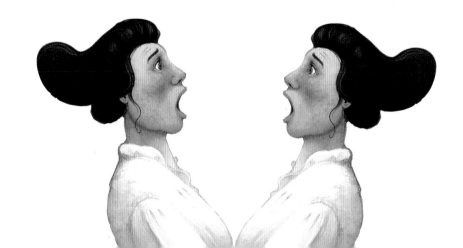

gaze
[gez]
動 凝視

stare
[stɛr]
動 盯著看

在一個春天的早晨，幾隻小羊要到田野去，途中經過農場大門。佩葛蒂和平常一樣，在水池邊凝視自己的倒影。小羊停下來，盯著佩葛蒂看。他們很滿意自己身上剛長出來的羊毛，但是什麼禮貌也不懂。其中一隻小羊說：

「你們看那隻老肥豬！」

「看她那呼嚕怪響的大鼻子。」

「她好醜哦！」他們說。

佩葛蒂剛開始沒聽到小羊說的話，直到有隻小羊咩咩咩地唱起歌來，其他的也跟著一起唱：

「醜老豬，臭兮兮，紅不溜丟肥嘟嘟，全身光溜溜！」

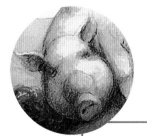

bleat
[blit]
動 （羊）咩咩叫

bald
[bɔld]
形 光溜溜的

The lambs ran off laughing, leaving
Peggoty to gaze at her reflection.
Instead of the prettiest, pinkest, most
perfect pig, she now saw that she
was truly and **awfully** ugly. And not
only ugly, but **bald** as well!

A tear **trickled** down her snout
and **plopped** into the duckpond.
Why had she been born bald? There
must have been some mistake. She
dried her eyes and decided to ask the
wise old horse who knew about such things.

instead of...
代替…

awfully
[ˋɔflɪ]
副 驚人地

小羊嘻鬧地跑掉了，只剩佩葛蒂自個兒凝視著倒影。她現在看到的自己不再是最漂亮、最粉嫩、最完美，反而是奇醜無比。不但醜，全身還光溜溜的！
眼淚沿著鼻子滑落，啪地一聲滴落到池塘裡。為什麼她生下來就沒有毛呢？一定有什麼地方弄錯了！佩葛蒂擦乾眼淚，決定去問聰明的馬伯伯，這些事他都懂。

trickle
[ˋtrɪkl]
動 滴，流

plop
[plɑp]
動 撲通落下

12

13

She found the wise old horse **munching** hay in the barn.
"Excuse me," said Peggoty, most **politely**, "but could you tell me why I am bald?"

"Bald? Ah yes," said the wise old horse, who spoke **horribly** slow.

"The reason you're bald is perfectly **plain**. They must have forgotten to give you a **mane**."

"And please, is that what makes me so awfully ugly?" asked Peggoty.

"Why of course," said the horse, "there is no finer thing in all the world than a **glossy** and **galloping** mane."

Peggoty **trotted** into the yard where she met….

munch
[mʌntʃ]
動 大聲咀嚼

politely
[pə`laɪtlɪ]
副 客氣地

horribly
[`hɔrəblɪ]
副 非常地

plain
[plen]
形 清楚的

mane
[men]
图 鬃毛

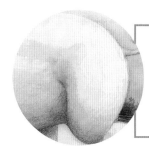

glossy
[`glɔsɪ]
形 有光澤的

佩葛蒂找到聰明的馬伯伯，他正在穀倉裡嚼著稻草。

她十分客氣地說：「對不起！您可不可以告訴我為什麼我身上沒有毛呢？」

「沒有毛？嗯！」馬伯伯慢吞吞地回答，「妳身上沒有毛的原因其實很簡單，一定是他們忘了在妳身上加些鬃毛了！」

「這就是我這麼醜的原因嗎？」佩葛蒂問。

「那當然囉！」馬伯伯說，「全世界沒有任何東西比得上光滑柔亮、奔跑時會在風中飛揚的鬃毛了。」

佩葛蒂快步跑到庭院，結果遇見了……

galloping
[`gæləpɪŋ]
形 飛奔的

trot
[trat]
動 快步

...the **marmalade** cat, **curled up** in the **shade**.

"Excuse me," said Peggoty, most politely, "but do you know why I am bald?"

The marmalade cat opened one eye and looked at Peggoty. "The reason you're bald is right under your nose.

You're wearing no fur from your tail to your toes."

Peggoty nodded sadly. "And is that what makes me so awfully ugly?"

"Of course," **purred** the cat, "there is no finer thing in the world than lickable, tickable fur."

marmalade
[ˋmarml͵ed]
名 果醬黃

curl up
蜷縮

全身橘黃色的貓咪，蜷縮著身子窩在樹蔭下。

「對不起，」佩葛蒂非常有禮貌地問：「你知道為什麼我身上光溜溜的嗎？」

橘黃貓睜開一隻眼睛，看著佩葛蒂說：「妳身上光溜溜的答案就在眼前，因為妳全身上下都沒有軟毛。」

佩葛蒂難過地點點頭。「這就是我那麼醜的原因嗎？」

「沒錯，」貓咪喵喵地說，「世界上沒有什麼東西比得過可以用舌頭去舔、還可以把身體包裹起來的軟毛。」

shade
[ʃed]
名 陰暗處

purr
[pɝ]
動 （貓）喵喵叫

For the rest of that day Peggoty hid herself from the other animals.
It was after dark when she returned to the humble, tumbledown barn. Only the moon was out.

"Oh **luminous** moon," **sighed** Peggoty, "why was I born so bald and awfully ugly?"

To her great **surprise** a voice sang back,
"The reason is perfectly simple to sing.
You have no feathers on either wing."
Peggoty looked up. It wasn't the moon talking after all, it was the singing cock on the roof.

luminous
[`lumənəs]
形 明亮的

後來，佩葛蒂就躲著其他的動物，一直到天黑以後，她才回去那座破舊、半倒的穀倉。外頭除了月亮，什麼都沒有。
「哦！皎潔的明月呀！」佩葛蒂嘆了口氣說：「為什麼我生下來就沒有毛，又這麼醜呢？」
突然有個聲音從背後響起，把佩葛蒂嚇了一大跳。
「這個問題太容易回答了！那是因為妳的翅膀上連根羽毛也沒有。」
佩葛蒂抬頭一看，原來不是月亮在說話，而是在屋頂上唱歌的那隻公雞。

sigh
[saɪ]
動 嘆氣

surprise
[sə`praɪz]
名 驚訝

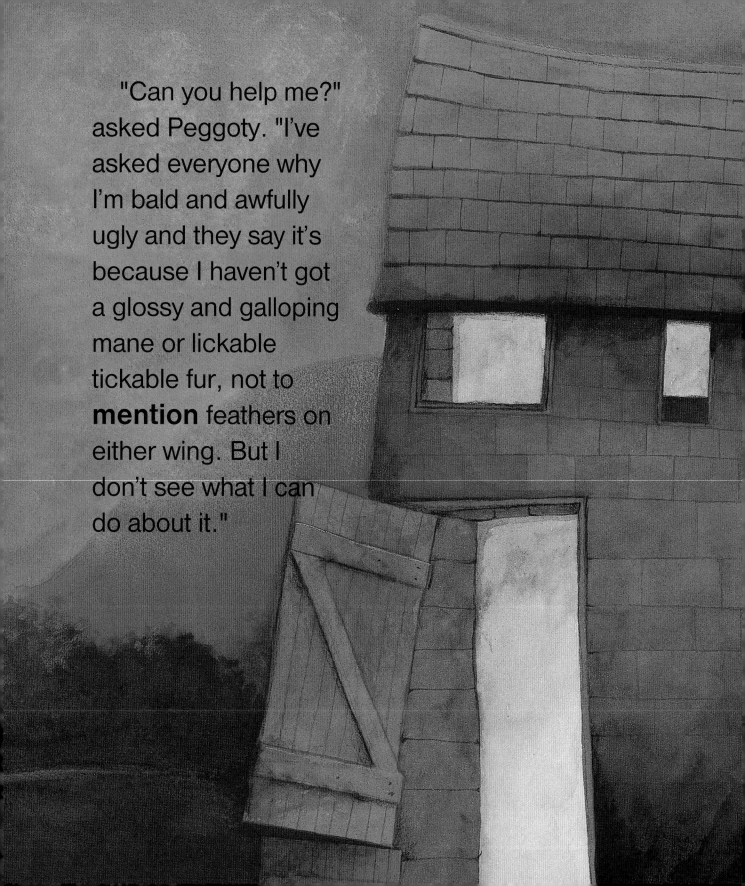

"Can you help me?" asked Peggoty. "I've asked everyone why I'm bald and awfully ugly and they say it's because I haven't got a glossy and galloping mane or lickable tickable fur, not to **mention** feathers on either wing. But I don't see what I can do about it."

The cock **strutted** up
and down on the roof.
It sang:
"*It would* **indeed** *be a strange
and wonderful* **sight**,
*If a pig could grow feathers
overnight.*"

「你可以幫幫我嗎？」佩葛蒂問。「我已經問過大家，為什麼我長得光溜溜、醜哩呱嘰的。他們說那是因為我沒有光滑柔亮、奔跑時會在風中飛揚的鬃毛，也沒有可以用舌頭去舔、還可以把身體包裹起來的軟毛，更別說長在翅膀上的羽毛了。可是我還是不知道應該怎麼辦才好？」

公雞在屋頂上裝腔作勢地走來走去，然後唱著：

「如果有小豬能在一夜之間長出羽毛，那可真是奇怪又奇妙！」

Suddenly Peggoty's tail began to **twitch** the way it did when she had an idea. Without **bidding** the singing cock goodnight, she ran into the barn.

All that night, while the other animals slept, strange **rustling** and **scuffling** sounds came from Peggoty's corner.

twitch
[twɪtʃ]
勔 猛然抽動

bid
[bɪd]
勔 說

突然，佩葛蒂的尾巴抽動了一下，就像平常她想到了什麼點子一樣。沒跟唱歌的公雞說聲晚安，她便跑回了穀倉。
整個晚上，其他動物都在睡覺，可是從佩葛蒂的角落不斷傳出窸窸窣窣、乒乒乓乓的奇怪聲音。

rustling
[`rʌslɪŋ]
圃 窸窣作響的

scuffle
[`skʌfl]
勔 扭打成一團

When the first sunlight **crept** into the barn, the cock **crowed** and the animals came out into the yard. Everyone stared at Peggoty. Overnight she had grown hair. Golden **locks** of hair as curly as a pig's tail. Peggoty **tossed** her head proudly and **paraded** in front of them.

creep
[krip]
動 悄悄來到

crow
[kro]
動 啼叫

lock
[lɑk]
名 鬈髮

當第一道陽光悄悄照入穀倉的時候，公雞喔喔叫著，動物們都走出穀倉，來到庭院。大家吃驚地看著佩葛蒂。一夜之間，她長出頭髮來了，像豬尾巴那樣捲的捲髮。佩葛蒂昂首闊步從大家面前走過。

toss
[tɔs]
動 抬起

parade
[pə`red]
動 炫耀

Just then the young lambs passed by
the gate, following their mother
up to the fields.

"Look at the pig!" shouted one.

"What's she got on her head?"
"The pig is wearing a **wig**!" they cried.

They all crowded around the gate,
bleating and **giggling** at poor Peggoty.
"The pig is wearing a wig! The pig is
wearing a wig!" they sang.

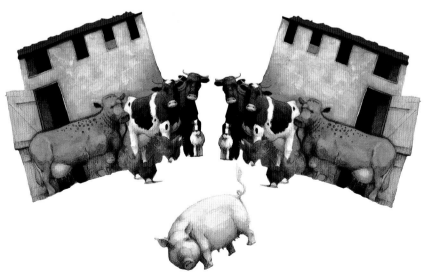

wig
[wɪg]
名 假髮

就在這個時候，那群小羊跟著媽媽要到田野裡去，正巧又經過了大門。

「看那隻豬！」一隻小羊叫著。

「她頭上長什麼東西呀？」

「小豬戴假髮呢！」其他小羊叫著。

他們全擠在門口，咩咩咩、咯咯咯地嘲笑可憐的佩葛蒂。

「小豬戴假髮！小豬戴假髮！」小羊一起唱著。

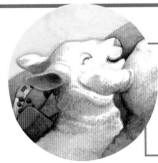

giggle
[ˋgɪgl̩]
動 咯咯笑

Peggoty's pink face turned red. She took to her **trotters** and **fled** up the hill. She didn't stop running until she reached the big farmhouse at the top. There she crept into the **shadow** of the wall and **wept**. Tears ran down her **plump** cheeks and the straw wig sat **crooked** and **crumpled** on her head.

trotter
[`trɑtɚ]
名 （豬的）腳

flee
[fli]
動 逃離

shadow
[`ʃædo]
名 陰影

weep
[wip]
動 （不出聲地）哭

plump
[plʌmp]
形 圓胖的

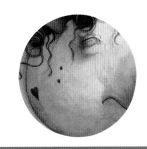

佩葛蒂粉紅色的臉漲得通紅。她拔腿就往山丘上跑去，一直跑到山頂上的大農莊，才停了下來。她悄悄地走到牆蔭下，啜泣著。眼淚從她圓鼓鼓的臉頰滾落下來，稻草做的假髮捲曲塌亂地散落在她的頭上。

crooked
[ˋkrʊkɪd]
形 歪斜的

crumpled
[ˋkrʌmpl̩d]
形 皺巴巴的

"Waah haah!" a voice **wailed** nearby.
Peggoty **sniffed** and listened.
Someone else was crying too.
It was coming from the farmhouse.

Hush, hush, my poppsie!
Don't cry, my **precious**,"
she sang.

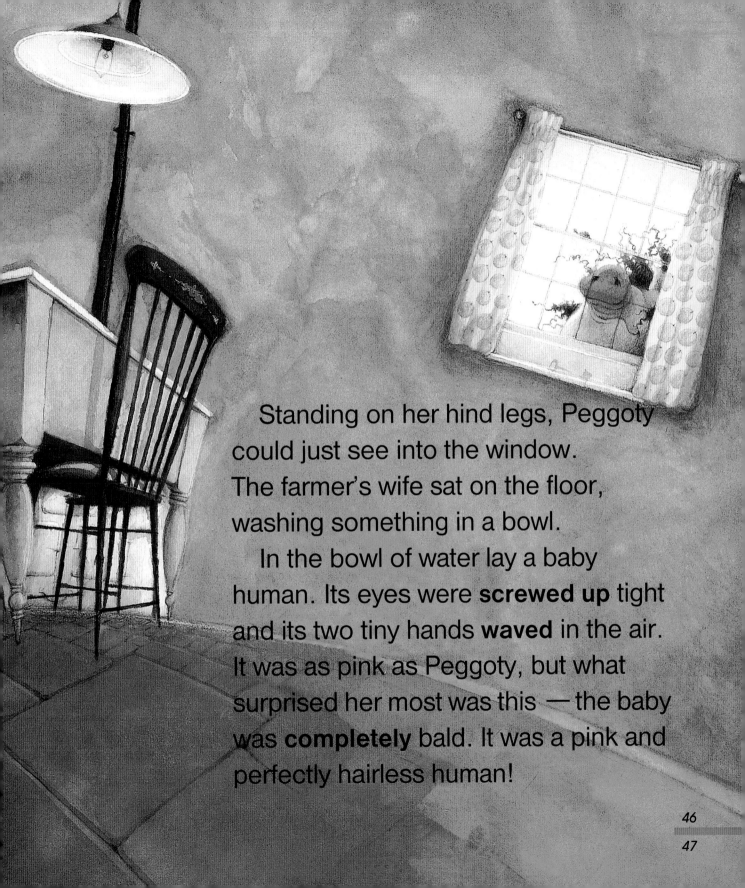

Standing on her hind legs, Peggoty could just see into the window. The farmer's wife sat on the floor, washing something in a bowl.

In the bowl of water lay a baby human. Its eyes were **screwed up** tight and its two tiny hands **waved** in the air. It was as pink as Peggoty, but what surprised her most was this — the baby was **completely** bald. It was a pink and perfectly hairless human!

wail
[wel]
動 哭號

sniff
[snɪf]
動 嗅

precious
[ˋprɛʃəs]
名 寶貝

「哇！哇！」附近傳來一陣哭啼聲。佩葛蒂聞了又聞，聽了又聽。還有別人在哭呢！聲音從農舍傳了出來。

「噓！噓！我的小親親。不哭，我的小寶貝。」她哄唱著。

佩葛蒂踮起後腳，剛好可以看到窗戶裡面。農場主人的太太坐在地板上，洗著水盆裡的東西。

水盆裡躺著一個小嬰兒，雙眼緊閉，兩隻小手在空中揮舞。它跟佩葛蒂一樣，都是粉嫩嫩的，不過她最驚訝的是：小嬰兒竟然全身光溜溜的。一個粉紅色、全身都沒有毛的人類！

wave
[wev]
動 揮動

completely
[kəm`plitlɪ]
副 完全地

48
49

The farmer's wife **tickled** the baby's round **tummy**.
"You're bootiful. My bootiful angel," she **cooed**.
The baby began to **gurgle** and giggle. Peggoty
pressed her face against the glass, smiling back.
At that moment the farmer's wife looked up and
saw the **bedraggled**, **bewigged** face at her window.

"HELP!" she screamed. "A horrible hairy **monster**!"
    Peggoty fell over backward with
fright. The crooked and crumpled wig
fell off. She left it in the mud and ran
out through the gate and back down
the hill.

tickle
[ˋtɪkl̩]
動 搔癢

tummy
[ˋtʌmɪ]
名 肚子

coo
[ku]
動 輕聲地說

gurgle
[ˋgɝgl̩]
動 發出咯咯聲

農場主人的太太在小嬰兒圓圓的肚子搔癢。

「你真漂亮！我美麗的小天使！」她輕聲說。

嬰兒開始發出咯咯的笑聲。佩葛蒂的臉緊貼著窗戶玻璃，露出微笑。

這時候，農場主人的太太抬起頭，看見窗口佩葛蒂髒髒亂亂、戴著假髮的臉。

「救命啊！」她尖叫起來，「毛茸茸的怪物！」

佩葛蒂害怕地往後退。捲曲塌亂的假髮掉在泥濘中。佩葛蒂穿過大門，跑下山丘。

That night she told her story to the other animals in the humble, tumbledown barn.

"And so," she **concluded**, "if you are hairy, humans think you are a horrible hairy monster, but if you are bald (and here she **blushed modestly**) they call you a bootiful angel."

conclude
[kən`klud]
動 下結論

當天晚上，佩葛蒂在那破破爛爛、半倒的穀倉裡，把她的見聞說給動物們聽。「所以，」她的結論是，「如果你全身毛茸茸的，人類會認為你是可怕的怪物。可是如果你身上光溜溜的，（說到這裡，她的臉不好意思地紅了起來），他們會說你是美麗的小天使呢！」

blush
[blʌʃ]
動 臉紅

modestly
[`mɑdɪstlɪ]
副 羞怯地

Peggoty has never worn a wig since that day. And she doesn't believe that the finest thing in all the world is a glossy and galloping mane, lickable tickable fur, or feathers on either wing. She thinks that pigs are born just perfect.

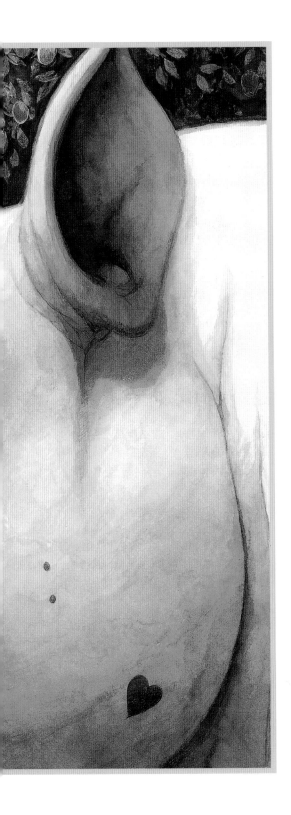

從此以後，佩葛蒂再也不戴假髮了。她不相信世界上最好的東西是光滑柔亮、奔跑時會在風中飛揚的鬃毛，或是可以用舌頭去舔、可以把身體包裹起來的軟毛，或是長在翅膀上的羽毛。她認為小豬天生就是完美無瑕的。

別害怕！羊咩咩！

羊咩咩最討厭夜晚了，
到處黑漆漆的，
還有很多恐怖的黑影子，
而且其中一個黑影子
老是跟在他後面……
羊咩咩怎樣才能不再害怕黑影子呢？

農場裡的小故事

快快睡！豬小弟！

上床時間到了，
豬小弟還不肯睡，
他還想到處玩耍，
可是大家都不理他，
他只好自己玩……

有一個農場，
裡面住著怕黑的羊咩咩、
不肯睡覺的豬小弟、
愛搗蛋的斑斑貓

和愛咯咯叫的小母雞，
農場主人真是煩惱啊！
他到底要怎麼解決
這些寶貝蛋的問題呢？

別吵了！小母雞！

小母雞最愛咯咯叫，
吵得大家受不了，
誰可以想個好法子，
讓她不再吵鬧？

別貪心！斑斑貓！

斑斑貓最壞了，搶走了小狗狗的玩具球，
扯掉豬小弟的蝴蝶結，
還吃光了農夫的便當……
她會受到什麼樣的教訓呢？

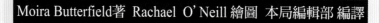

Moira Butterfield 著　Rachael O'Neill 繪圖　本局編輯部 編譯

國家圖書館出版品預行編目資料

小豬戴假髮 = The pig in a wig / Alan MacDonald 著；
Paul Hess 繪；施純宜譯－－初版．－－臺北市：
三民，民88
　面；　公分
ISBN 957–14–3002–1（平裝）

1.英國語言－讀本

805.18　　　　　　　　　　　　　88004008

網際網路位址　http : // www. sanmin. com. tw

ⓒ 小豬戴假髮

著作人　Alan MacDonald
繪圖者　Paul Hess
譯　者　施純宜
發行人　劉振強
著作財　三民書局股份有限公司
產權人
　　　　臺北市復興北路三八六號
發行所　三民書局股份有限公司
　　　　地址／臺北市復興北路三八六號
　　　　電話／二五○○六六○○
　　　　郵撥／○○○九九九八——五號
印刷所　三民書局股份有限公司
門市部　復北店／臺北市復興北路三八六號
　　　　重南店／臺北市重慶南路一段六十一號
初　版　中華民國八十八年十一月
編　號　S85459
定　價　新臺幣貳佰元整
行政院新聞局登記證局版臺業字第○二○○號

ISBN　957–14–3002–1（平裝）